To Mike and Charlotte –*C.P.*
For Gregory and Donatella –*V.V.*

tiger tales
an imprint of ME Media, LLC
202 Old Ridgefield Road, Wilton, CT 06897
Published in the United States 2011
Originally published 2009 as *Beckett and the Panda-monium*
Text copyright © 2009 Cynthia Platt
Illustrations copyright © 2009 Veronica Vasylenko
The illustrated depiction of Ty Inc. plush toys are used with the permission of Ty Inc.
© 2009, Ty Inc. All rights reserved. TY, The Ty Heart Logo, TY CLASSIC and BECKETT
are all federally registered trademarks owned by Ty Inc. Visit Ty at www.ty.com
CIP data is available
Hardcover ISBN-13: 978-1-58925-093-2
Hardcover ISBN-10: 1-58925-093-1
Paperback ISBN-13: 978-1-58925-425-1
Paperback ISBN-10: 1-58925-425-2
Printed in China
LPP 0610
All rights reserved
1 3 5 7 9 10 8 6 4 2

For more insight and activities, visit us at **www.tigertalesbooks.com**

PANDA-MONIUM!

by Cynthia Platt

Illustrated by Veronica Vasylenko

tiger tales

Little Beckett was a panda
feeling rather blue.
Empty tummy **rumbling**,
he needed some bamboo.
He really needed **crunchy**, **munchy**
sweet bamboo to chew!

So up the hill, with a big bear **stomp**,
Beckett searched for snacks to chomp.

Soon two pandas saw little Beckett
looking for snacks to chew.
They watched as Beckett strolled along
singing a happy bamboo song.
Those other pandas really liked his song
about bamboo!

And then, without a warning,
they were feeling hungry, too—
for hard and ripe, fun to swipe
sweet bamboo to chew.

So down the hill, they promptly rolled
to follow Beckett as he strolled.

Little Beckett—with two pandas—
walked where lilies grew.
And on those flower beds
woke three panda sleepyheads.
Those pandas had been dreaming
   such sweet dreams about bamboo!

And it comes as no surprise,
they were feeling hungry, too—
for tasty, green, **long** and lean
sweet bamboo to chew.

So from the flowers, pandas slipped—
off searching for bamboo they **skipped**.

Little Beckett—with five pandas—
marched through forests, too.
He didn't see four pandas there
in a game of **leap**-the-**bear.**
But all that leaping gets a panda
  thinking of bamboo!

They very quickly realized
they were feeling hungry, too—
for tall and wobbly, fun and gobbly
sweet bamboo to chew.

And with their jumping game now done,
they joined the others at a run.

Little Beckett walked through brambles
with a **HUGE** panda crew.
Four pandas were hiding and peeking.
Another, so slyly, was seeking—
but hide-and-seek got those five pandas
   yearning for bamboo!

When out of hiding they all came,
their cravings grew and grew—
for hard, delicious, so nutritious
sweet bamboo to chew.

So, picking brambles from their fur,
they followed Beckett in a **blur**.

Little Beckett was a panda,
who thought he was alone.
He didn't know that right behind him,
panda crowds had grown.

So when he climbed a ginkgo tree
to look for sweet bamboo,
a hungry horde of giant pandas
climbed right up there, too!

The tree began to **shimmy**,
the tree rocked to and fro,
and all those hungry panda bears ...

bounced out high and low.

It was **PANDA-MONIUM!**

The bears rolled here, the bears rolled there,
they tumbled quickly by.
Little Beckett **bumped** and **thumped**,
and heaved a panda sigh.
He worried that he just might NEVER find
    some sweet bamboo!

And yet, as Beckett **bounced** and **flew**,
he thought that he could smell . . .

BAMBOO!

Little Beckett was a panda
no longer feeling blue.
Empty tummy **rumbling**,
he landed in bamboo!
Some **crunch** and **munch**, time for lunch,
green bamboo to chew.

So, all alone, he took a seat—
to have some sweet bamboo to eat!